THE STATE OF SIEGE

The *Strangers and Brothers*
novel sequence by
C. P. SNOW

C. P. SNOW
is also the author of

C. P. Snow

THE STATE
OF SIEGE

The John Findley Green
Foundation Lectures
Westminster College
November 1968

CHARLES SCRIBNER'S SONS
New York

The John Findley Green Foundation was established by the late Mrs. Green in 1937 as a memorial to her husband, who was a graduate of Westminster College in the Class of 1884 and served as a member of the college's Board of Trustees for twenty-seven years.

The Deed of Gift provides for lectures "by a man of international reputation, whose topic selected by himself . . . shall promote understanding of economic, political, and social problems of international concern."

THE STATE OF SIEGE

᪣ I ᪣

Last year, 1967, I traveled a good many thousand miles. This was partly out of duty and partly out of curiosity, but the reasons don't matter. The fact was, I came twice to North America, Canada as well as the United States. I also went twice to the Soviet Union, on one trip almost the whole length —though not the breadth—from the Baltic coast down to Georgia. On the way back, I stayed in Poland. And I paid another call, a little nearer home, to Scandinavian countries.

On all those journeys, as you would expect, I had a lot of conversations with friends and acquaintances. Many of them are people I have known for ten or twenty years. At the end of it all, when I was back in London in the fall, just a year ago, I was left with one overmastering impression. Nearly everyone was worried about our world and what was happening to it. Nearly everyone was uncertain about the future. There was more—I don't want to use too strong a word—uneasiness in the air than I could remember. And it was an uneasiness that I understood, that I couldn't precisely define but without question shared.

I ought to make one or two qualifications. Like anyone of my age, I had known times when people round me had been more desperately and immediately concerned. That was true in the '30s in Europe. It was true, of course, in London in 1940 and further on into the war. But then the causes of concern were not in the least mysterious, long-distance, or obscure. There was usually something for one to do, it might be tiny or ineffective, but it took one's mind away. It was possible to hope for the end of the war, and a better time afterwards. It was possible to hope, not in a utopian fashion, but as most healthy people always want to hope.

Those situations were quite unlike the present one. Those concerns were quite unlike the present uneasiness. This is harder to shift, more impalpable, nothing like so obvious. It isn't exactly unhappiness or dread. Many of the persons I listened to last year were entirely happy in their private lives. Some were not, it goes without saying: some were ill, or had illness close to them, or the other fatalities that afflict us all. It doesn't need explanation that they should be in distress. But it does ask for explanation that robust and happy people, of different ages, in different societies, should feel an uneasiness that they can't shake off. Uneasiness which seems to be becoming part of the climate of our time. Uneasiness with an edge of fear? Perhaps. It is a bad state. It can be a paralyzing and self-destructive state. If I had been making the same journeys this year instead of last, I am certain that I should have felt that this uneasiness was deepening: just as I have felt it in myself.

What is going wrong with us? Of course, we are not the first people in history to have this kind of experience or ask this kind of question. But we can deal only with our own time and speak only with our own words. It does seem—and though the feeling is subjective it is strong and one can hear it expressed by the very young—that our world is closing in. It gives us the sensation of contracting, not of expanding. This is very odd. It is very odd intellectually. For, after all, ours is the time of all times when men have performed some of their greatest triumphs. It is, or ought to be, exciting that there will soon be the first voyage round the moon: that is a technical triumph, and for many, I suspect, a release from some of our day-by-day unease. What for me is more exciting are the supreme intellectual triumphs which we are not very far from witnessing. I can remember, in Cambridge in 1932, hearing at a private gathering the first news of the discovery of the neutron. That doesn't sound dramatic: but it was extremely dramatic. From it flowed all the fantastic Alice-in-Wonderland universe of particle physics, the extraordinary collection of tiny bits which make up what we call matter. For a generation that collection has become more complicated and at times it has looked intolerably untidy. Now at last the theoretical physicists may be within touching distance of a new order—something which is still complex, but as beautiful and as revolutionary for the micro-universe as Copernicus's scheme was for the solar system. If that happens—and the betting in favor is quite heavy—it will be one of the supreme achievements of the human mind.

I can also remember, in Cambridge about the same time, listening to some of the first discussions about a new branch of science. That new branch we have now come to know as molecular biology. Remember that the first pioneering work started only thirty-odd years ago: and think what has happened since. DNA. The mechanism of heredity. The genetic code. The physical structure of life itself. In the whole of scientific history, there have been perhaps half a dozen breakthroughs which signified as much. And, like all real breakthroughs, the significance is going to seep into us more deeply year after year. That was true with Darwin's revolution. So it is, and perhaps more startlingly, today. It is likely that before long we shall be told of the making, in the laboratory, of a living cell.

These wonderful things have been done, and are being done, in our own time, by people like ourselves. If you read James Watson's book *The Double Helix* you will realize that they are remarkably like ourselves. With most of our frailties and with a similar component of original sin. But they have done these things, and that ought to make us feel proud to be living at this time, and to belong to the same species. Yet are we? I think only partially. We are not very good at counting our blessings. That is a feature of our particular uneasiness. And also we suspect, and we have some right to suspect, that for these great intellectual triumphs we shall pay a price. We can't enjoy our knowledge and our understanding as unself-consciously and innocently as once we did. Upon us all there lies the shadow of Dr. Faust: or, to be concrete, the shadow of the cloud over Hiroshima.

To some extent, those suspicions (which are really a distrust of the whole human race) show a failure of nerve. To an almost equal extent, they are essential: essential, that is, if we are ever going to build a tolerable world. I shall come back to that point later. At any rate, the suspicions exist. They prevent the most supreme achievements of our time giving us the liberation that they might have done. They may alleviate, but they do not stop, the pressure of a world closing in.

The world closes in. We are bombarded with communications, but again those don't set us free. Television has probably affected the pattern of our lives more than any other technical device—including the automobile and the telephone. Television bombards us with communications about the world outside—often unpleasant, often (at least in the television of the West) horrific. We know incomparably more than any human beings before us about what is going on in other cities, in other countries. Particularly the immediate prospect of human suffering. We know it is happening. We see people starving before they have died: we know that they are going to die. We see the evening's killings in Mexico City the same evening in London. We see the victims of famine in Biafra. We know it all. We know so much: and we can do so little. We turn away. There may be an even more sinister effect, to which I shall return.

Yes, we turn away. We don't project ourselves

outwards: we turn inwards. We draw what in England we call the curtains, and we try to make an enclave of our own. An enclave, a refuge, a place to shut out the noise. A group of one's own. Enclave-making: that is one of the characteristic symptoms of our unease. You can see it plain in bigger and in smaller forms. Some of the bigger forms are cropping up right round the world. The revival of nationalisms, particularly of small nationalisms which had been half-dissolved in a more outward-looking age. Take my own small island. It would have seemed very curious not long ago to be told that a large proportion of the Scotch and Welsh are going to feel intense emotion about walling themselves off in little enclaves of their own. Incidentally making things very difficult for themselves in the process by, at least in Wales, immediately encouraging a first-rate language problem. Just as is happening in Belgium, one of the most prosperous and densely populated countries on earth: if there is any possibility of shutting ourselves off behind language walls, then, in our present mood, we rush to do so.

Further, one of the bigger forms of enclave-making, again all round the world, is the behavior of great strata of the young. They too have turned inwards: into their own customs, and often their own private language: often into a private fairyland where what some of them describe as "structures" do not exist. In essence, they are creating privacies, even those who go out in the streets: for once you try to dismiss structures, you are dismissing society, any kind of society, including primitive, advanced, or anarchist, and you are huddling into a private refuge of your own.

One could go on with the list of enclaves that we can see being built round us, or are building for ourselves. Race and color the most isolating of them all. But clearest of all are the smaller forms of this process. Those are the forms which so many of us are taking part in.

Let us be honest. Most of us are huddling together in our own little groups for comfort's sake. It is natural, of course, for people to like their like, and to be easier with those who have the same associations as themselves. Most people, as they get older, get support from those few they have known for a long time. That is natural. But we often use natural feelings as an excuse. We are turning inward more than is really natural. As I said before, we draw the curtains and take care not to listen to anything which is going on in the streets outside. We are behaving as though we were in a state of siege.

◈ II ◈

It doesn't need saying that there are some objective reasons, as well as psychological ones, why sensible persons in the cities of the advanced world should behave as though they were in a state of siege. The modern city, the city of the last third of our century, is not an entirely reposeful place to live in. For many of us, it has a certain charm. But it is no use pretending that it is much like classical Athens or sixteenth century Venice. It is a great deal healthier, if one's thinking of disease: on the other hand, in terms of murder and bodily harm, it is very much less physically safe. The advanced world has, we all know, become remarkably richer during the last thirty years. This is true of all industrialized countries, including the U.S.S.R. Poverty has been diminished to an extent that most of us couldn't have foreseen, and certainly didn't foresee. There is extremely little subsistence poverty, for example, in Scandinavia and Holland. Not much in my own country. Thirty years ago, it was a genial assumption that, once poverty had been effectively got rid of, so would most crime go too. Has it? In fact, even in countries where poverty is now minimal, crime is increasing by a good many per cent per year. Someone calculated, a few years ago, that at the current rate of production, the entire British population would by 2040 consist of scientists and criminals. Since that time, unfortunately, we have fallen behind in our production of scientists.

All this is hard to take. The relation between crime and poverty isn't a simple one. We don't know the Soviet crime statistics since they became more prosperous: there aren't many sets of figures which would be more interesting. But we do know the Western statistics. They are bizarre. It is true that, for several special reasons, the United States is not typical: the harsh fact is that American cities are, in criminal terms, the most lethal in the advanced world. Britain has under 200 murders a year, and the United States something like thirty times as many. But, even in comparatively nonlethal cities like London, or Stockholm, or Budapest, nevertheless there is enough crime surging round one—far more than a generation ago—to give some reason for a siege mentality. As I say, no one understands this exponential development of crime in rich countries. It may be that modern technology, on the whole, makes crime rather easier: and there are also some dark truths about human psychology, which perhaps we have been too complacent, or perhaps too kind to ourselves, to wish to see clearly.

Yet, though many of us do live in an environment with that undercurrent of anxiety, that isn't the whole story, or even an important part of it. The major unease is deeper, subtler, and perhaps less selfish. Why are we turning inwards? Many of us are lucky, luckier in material terms than any large numbers of men have ever been. Isn't it ridiculous, or plain cowardly, that we should let ourselves feel besieged? Yet, much of the time, we do.

There can't be one single unique cause for this condition. All we are inclined to do, according to our temperaments and our particular society, is pluck out from a whole complex of causes one which strikes our fancy—or more exactly one which touches a specially painful nerve. An obvious one is the increasing complicatedness and articulation of the modern industrial state. An articulation which is to a large extent independent of political systems and which has been produced inexorably as a result of the technological process itself. So that we really don't comprehend it, even those who boom most confidently about it. We feel as though we are in a motorbus driven very fast by a probably malevolent and certainly anonymous driver; we can't stop it, all we can do is show a stiff upper lip and pretend to smile at the passing countryside. There is no doubt that, to many people, this is a genuine response. It leads—because we like to invent names which excuse ourselves and make us seem less inadequate—to all the varieties of alienation and the existential absurd. It leads a good many to wish to return to an earlier and simpler society. About that, I'd lie to remark in passing that no society *when men have actually lived in it* has seemed as simple as it does looking back. The nineteenth century seemed distressingly complex to intelligent persons who were there: just read about Dickens' Mr. Merdle or Trollope's Mr. Melmotte. Dickens and Trollope were men of great experience: their worries were not all that dissimilar from ours, they didn't see their way through any more sharply, and they were writing a hundred years ago.

Still, the complicatedness of the 1968 society weighs upon many. That is one of many causes of our unease. Nuclear weapons, biological weapons, the power to wipe out so many human lives. That *is* novel and peculiar to our time, and it is another cause. Any of us can produce more such causes, none of them the total answer, all of them part of the truth. I am going to produce two now. They are not original, they have been said many times. Again, they are not the total answer. But they are important. They are interconnected. They are among the noises that we don't want to hear.

The first is the sheer scale of the human enterprise. In many places and for many purposes, including some of the fundamental human purposes, there are already too many people in the world. Within a generation, there will be far too many. Within two or three generations—unless we show more sense, goodwill and foresight than men have ever shown—there will be tragically too many. So many that the ordinary human hopes will have disappeared. Disappeared irreversibly, perhaps: or at least for so long that we can't imagine how they will emerge again.

This is an old story now. It has become a cliché, as Mr. McNamara said in September. As he also said, the trouble about clichés is not that they are untrue: often they are too terribly true. The trouble is, we stop listening to them. Incidentally, perhaps I might be allowed to mention my admiration for Mr. McNamara's statements. They are the bravest and most direct that any world statesman has made so far. He is more optimistic than I can find it within myself to be: but the President of the World Bank ought to be optimistic, while I am speaking as a private citizen.

Well, it is an old story. Everyone knows the brute facts. At the time of the first English settlements in America, there were something like half a billion human beings alive. When people still living were born, that figure, the population of the planet, would be round one billion. It is now, in 1968, well over three billion. By 2000 A.D. it will be over six billion, and may be nearer seven billion.

Some of our thoughtful forefathers used to have, somewhere where their eyes couldn't evade it, a human skull. *Memento mori.* A reminder that you too are going to die. I sometimes think that every politician and decision-maker in the world ought to have on his desk that graph of the human population. A reminder that they too are going to be born.

It is no use trying to comfort yourself by doubts about this kind of statistical projection. In detail, of course, such projections can go wrong. That is specifically true for advanced countries. Before 1939, for instance, the demographic curve for the U.K. was pointing down, not up, as though the population would even out at 30,000,000 by the end of the century. It is now well over 50,000,000, and looks like being 70,000,000 by A.D. 2000. And we all realize that the Japanese cut their birth rate in half between 1951 and 1961. But that was the conscious effort of a whole people, one of the most educated on earth, and also the one with the most unusual social discipline and history. Those are minor ripples in the gross statistical projections, and there isn't a responsible person who doubts that in thirty years there will be nearly twice as many human beings living in our world. That is the *least* that can happen. That figure can't be lowered by any of the steps that Mr. McNamara and other men of sense would wish to put into action tomorrow. So much is foredoomed. The *best* that can happen is that the increase will slow down, and that from A.D. 2000 on we begin to approach a limit. A limit which is low enough not to kill hope.

Doubling the world population in thirty years. That is something new in history. On a small scale, countries like the U.K., as they became industrialized, had rapid increases in population. The U.K. doubled its population between 1800 and 1850, and again between 1850 and 1900. We were relatively rich, and had the wheat fields of America to obtain food from. There has never been anything comparable on a world scale. And it is only happening because of one of those paradoxes and contradictions that keep tantalizing us as we try to think about the problems of our times. It is happening, in fact, because of our partial control over nature. It is not so much that more babies are being born: the point is, we are so much better at keeping people alive. Medicine has gone round the world, the poor world as well as the rich, quicker than anything else. Not only has infantile mortality been reduced everywhere (remember, our great-grandparents, even the privileged in the most privileged countries, took the death of children as an inevitable fact of existence): not only that, but the length of life is also increasing everywhere. That is a triumph, and any decent human being rejoices in it. But it is presenting us with a situation in some ways graver than we have known before, and one that we may not be able to control.

At this point I think I ought to make something like an apology or a confession. Nearly ten years ago I gave another lecture, which I called *The Two Cultures and the Scientific Revolution,* and which produced, and in fact still continues to produce, a certain amount of discussion. But the discussion has concentrated on what to me was a secondary matter. The primary intention—at least in my own mind—was to try to depict one of the major practical crises in the world, that is the gap between the rich and the poor countries, and to suggest certain ways of thinking, practical ways of thinking, which were needed before we could meet it. As you will soon notice, I am returning to this topic here and now. And I have tried to avoid distractions or provocations so that it is my own fault if I can't make myself understood.

In the *Two Cultures* lecture there was a curious and culpable omission. It is that for which I can acknowledge the guilt now. I was talking about world crises: and I made only the slightest of references to the growth of population. That wasn't out of ignorance. I knew the facts. It wasn't out of carelessness. It was deliberate. I didn't want this major problem to dominate the discussion. Partly because it seemed to me then to make social hope even more difficult: partly because I didn't want to hurt other people's religious sensibilities. The religious sensibilities of people whom I knew, respected and often loved; and of others whom I didn't know. I now believe that I was dead wrong, and seriously wrong on both counts. First, any social hope that is going to be any use against the darkness ahead will have to be based upon a knowledge of the worst: the worst of the practical facts, the worst in ourselves. It will have to be a harsh and difficult hope. We have never needed it more. Second, the situation is so grave that sensibilities of any kind, any of ours, any of those we respect but disagree with, have to take their chance. We are dealing with the species-life. That responsibility has to take first place.

In smallish ways, the pattern of population is already making itself felt. Certainly it is in parts of Europe, like England or Belgium. Or in Japan. Maybe not so much in the United States, though when one flies over your gigantic conurbations, one feels that men are happier when they have room to swing a cat round. The Soviet Union, in most of its expanse, is still a surprisingly empty country, and it is much harder for a Russian than an Englishman to get psychologically involved in the population flood, though intellectually, of course, plenty of them are.

I have a suspicion that this flood is already making us more callous about human life. As I said before, the rapidity and completeness of human communications are constantly presenting us with the sight of famine, suffering, violent death. We turn away, inside our safe drawing rooms. It may be that these communications themselves help to make us callous. And yet, perhaps also there is the unadmitted thought that human lives are plentiful beyond belief? I don't know. There is another paradox here. For, side by side with our major callousness—which is much harsher than that of people similar to ourselves at the beginning of this century—we show, in individual instances, a concern far more extreme than they ever felt. In my own country, for example, there was a depth of emotion which swept away the vestigial relics of capital punishment that still survived—which had come down to about half a dozen executions a year. These individual instances occupied an enormous amount of time, both parliamentary and private; they took up energy and outward-going feeling: much more, so far as I can estimate, than the hundreds of thousands of deaths by starvation in Biafra. Yet let us chalk up a point in our own favor: at times we do care.

At other times, even within our own societies, we cease to care to an almost pathological extent. Think for a moment of the numbers of people killed in and by automobiles. In the U.S.A. upwards of 50,000 a year. In the U.K. 6,000 or so. If that happened through a disease, there would be outcries, foundations, research. As it is, we take it as an act of God: without feeling: like so many schizophrenics. In my country, there was even loud protest against the introduction of stiffer laws to deal with drunken driving: as though driving when drunk was one of the more sacred rights of man. If there are sane, humane and reflective people living in a better world than ours in five hundred years, they will look back on some of our callousness with incredulity. Perhaps with pity too. They may understand our situation in a way that we are incapable of. They may say that we were overwhelmed by the population flood. Or that we were living in one of the most violent ages in history, and so lost both our nerve and a great deal of our human feeling.

Just one more indication of how much we are overwhelmed. There is no single person alive who can speak on matters of simple human decency, and be listened to by people of goodwill everywhere. To anyone who knew him, Einstein spoke with moral authority unlike anything that we had ever heard or will ever hear again. But he also spoke to many men. Someone described him, about twenty years ago, as the conscience of the world. That isn't too much of an exaggeration. His voice reached across the divides and confusions of our time. Now we have no Einstein. There is no man, and no group of men, who could conceivably be called the conscience of the world.

Maybe those smallish things I have just mentioned are pointers along our way. But now we can't avoid any longer the fundamental trouble we are moving into: the trouble which, in truth, we are already in. This has certainly contributed to our state of siege. Never mind our mental states, though. The trouble is elemental. It is the contrast between the rich countries of the world and the poor. The fact that half our fellow human beings are living at or below subsistence level. The fact that in the unlucky countries the population is growing faster than the food to keep it alive. The fact that we may be moving—perhaps in ten years —into large-scale famine.

◈ III ◈

I began by saying that when one travels in many different countries, one finds people sharing the same uneasiness. I might have pointed out that I was speaking, so far as first-hand knowledge goes, of the lucky countries of the world. Take a great arc through the northern hemisphere. North America. Almost the whole of Europe. The U.S.S.R. Japan. If that was the entire world, adding in a few additional fortunate pockets like Australasia, there wouldn't be much, at least in terms of the most simple animal fatalities, to worry about. These are the rich countries: which doesn't mean anything very sumptuous, but merely that the great majority of their populations have enough to eat, a place to live in, and perhaps, as a luxury, the chance to buy a newspaper occasionally, or even a book. That does not sound magnificent: but it is more than any big society has been able to provide for all its members until quite recently. Starvation was a danger in the background for our not-so-distant ancestors. Now we have forgotten about it: we have a knack of remembering only the pretty past. In the rich countries, food has ceased to be a problem. Industrialized agriculture has had its spectacular successes in the United States and Canada. If we wanted, we could grow more food. All over the northern hemisphere, population is rising relatively slowly: too fast for many amenities, but not fast enough to cause us the most brutal concerns. The lucky countries, if there were no others, could see a way clear.

Unfortunately, there are nearly twice as many

people in the poor countries as in the rich. Further, there will—nothing can stop it—be an extra billion people added to the world population in the next ten years. Of those, rather more than three-quarters will be added to the poor. All these statements, as Mr. McNamara remarked with great force, are clichés. A lot of us—and most urgently of all, American demographers and food scientists—have been uttering them for years past. Here is another. The gap between the rich and poor countries is growing. Take the average daily income in a large slice of the poor countries. It is something like thirty-five cents a day. The average daily income in the U.S. is about eight dollars a day. Twenty times greater. In ten years it is likely to be thirty times greater.

Yes, those statements are clichés all right. Some of them are dreadful clichés: and I am using dreadful in its first meaning, that is full of dread. The most dreadful of all—again, men of sober judgment have been saying it for years—is that many millions of people in the poor countries are going to starve to death before our eyes—or, to complete the domestic picture, we shall see them doing so upon our television sets.

How soon? How many deaths? Can they be prevented? Can they be minimized?

Those are the most important questions in our world today. Much more important than all the things which fret us in Western societies—student power, racial conflicts, the disaffection of the young. Though I believe there is an invisible connection between our local problems and the catastrophic world one.

To answer those questions we have to rely to an extent upon judgment—which is really informed guessing. Most of the expert demographers and the agronomists take the most pessimistic view. It is usually right, in matters of judgment, to take a pessimistic view—so long as it doesn't inhibit one totally from action, even inadequate action. That is a lesson which we have all learned who have had any experience of war. But I want to stress that neither the extent of this catastrophe, nor the time it will happen, nor whether it will go on indefinitely or be controlled, can be precisely calculated. There are too many unknowns. One of the unknowns, or half-knowns, gives a glimmer of partial hope. I shall deal with that shortly. The only contribution I can make is to give my own judgment, for what it is worth. It is worth only as much or as little as anyone else's who can read the evidence. I am neither a demographer nor an agronomist. And there are different stresses of opinion among those who know most, and some areas of disagreement.

It is common ground that in large parts of the poor world, in sections of Asia, Africa, Latin America, the collision between rising population and available food is very near. The demographers say that there is no method of curtailing population growth within ten years. With great good fortune, and world effort, a little might just conceivably be done in twenty or thirty years. They call on the agronomists to pull something out of the bag to give the demographers enough time. The agronomists—or a large proportion of them—make exactly the same demand in reverse. Can the demographers reduce the human increase soon enough to give *them*—the people working on tropical agriculture—enough time?

Most informed opinion believes that neither step is going to happen in time: that is, the collision is going to take place. At best, this will mean local famines to begin with. At worst, the local famines will spread into a sea of hunger. The usual date predicted for the beginning of the local famines is 1975–80.

The only rational ground for putting this date further into the future is the hope of increasing food production. In fact, this is the chief area of disagreement between responsible men. Here, as it happens, there is the glimmer, the ray of hope, that I mentioned. In the midst of the bleak prospect, there is one genuine piece—though in the long term it mustn't be overestimated—of good news.

On July 17 the Indian Government issued a special postage stamp. It was a stamp to celebrate the wheat revolution. Stamps have been issued for many worse celebrations: it is very hard to think of a better. We have had some gloomy figures in this discussion. Let us have one heartening one. In the 1967–8 season, the wheat harvest in India was 17,000,000 metric tons. In 1964–5, which had better weather, the harvest was 12,000,000 metric tons. Very nearly the same increase, and the same kind of record harvest, has been grown in Pakistan. For the moment, the fear of hunger has been beaten back from the subcontinent.

This is a success story, carefully planned, and the result of many years' work. A great deal of the credit, and it is pleasant to say it here in the middle of the United States, goes to two great private foundations, the Rockefeller and the Ford. In 1942 —note how long ago—the Rockefeller Foundation provided the finance and encouragement for the International Center for the Improvement of

Wheat and Maize, set up in Mexico. The Ford Foundation now provides half this center's funds. The budget, interestingly enough, is not very large, under a million dollars a year: but the real secret has been the scientific insight. Dwarf wheat strains have been developed which have a high degree of resistance to tropical conditions. That took getting on for twenty years. In 1962 the Indians decided their best chance was to import those wheat strains. Their own research workers have introduced other genetic characteristics into them. The Pakistani did precisely the same two years later, and produced their own Mexipak strain. Both countries have shown great efficiency in educating their farmers. The results would have seemed impossible as recently as five years ago. The Rockefeller and Ford administrations, the scientists, their Indian and Pakistani colleagues have done more concrete good to our world than is given to most men. If I were an elector to the Nobel Peace Prize, my vote would go to them.

Something of the same nature, again supported by the two foundations, is happening to rice. There is an International Rice Research Institute in the Philippines, which started in 1962 and has been producing a high-yielding and disease-resisting strain of rice. The most promising one, called

IR8, has already been exported to Asia and South America. With any luck, more hunger will be pushed back for a while.

Well, this is good news. In making one's judgment of the future, it is a factor. We mustn't lose our heads, one way or the other. The limits to food production, even when as deeply planned as this, seem to be quite sharp. The population increase has no such limits. The collision is still on. The guess I should now make—as I said, this is no more useful than that of anyone else who reads the evidence—is that large-scale famine won't happen as early as 1975–80. There will probably (it is a bitter thing to say) be serious local famines, in, for instance, Latin America and parts of Africa. The major catastrophe will happen before the end of the century. We shall, in the rich countries, be surrounded by a sea of famine, involving hundreds of millions of human beings, unless three tremendous social tasks are by then in operation. Not just one alone, but all three. They are:

1] a concerted effort by the rich countries to produce food, money and technical assistance for the poor.

2] an effort by the poor countries themselves, on the lines of India and Pakistan, to revolutionize their food production.

3] an effort by the poor countries—with all the

assistance that can be provided under [1]—
to reduce or stop their population increase:
with a corresponding reduction in the population increase in the rich countries also.
Those are the three conditions, all necessary, if we
are to avoid social despair.

ஃ IV ௸

Despair is a sin. Or, if you talk in secular terms as
I do, it prevents one taking such action as one
might, however small it is. I have to say that I
have been nearer to despair this year, 1968, than
ever in my life. With the one exception that I have
just mentioned, about which we all had an intima-
tion before this year, everything that has happened
in public has pointed in the direction of anti-hope.
In 1967 one could feel this in the air. This year
one can see it.

I don't mean anything at all subtle. It goes without saying that to avoid major war, there has to be
some sort of understanding between the U.S. and
the U.S.S.R. It also goes without saying, I suggest,
that to avoid the catastrophe I have just been dis-

cussing—the catastrophe a little further ahead—there has to be something more than uneasy understanding, something more positive than coexistence, between the two great power centers of the world.

As for major war, I ought to say at once that in my view the chances are very much against. These may be famous last words, or rather words not specially famous because no one is left to know them. But major war—in the sense of a thermonuclear war between the two superpowers—has in fact been most unlikely for a good many years. Great countries don't usually commit mass suicide. The military understanding has been worked out. The balance of power has remained steady. I believe, as I shall say in a minute, that both countries will spend increasing sums on armaments. But the balance of power will still remain pretty steady. The risk of major war will be there, but it is small, and probably the least of our worries. Minor wars, and dangerous minor wars, will occur during the thirty years we are looking ahead. In some of these, nuclear weapons may be used. But even that will not produce the mutual elimination of the United States and the U.S.S.R. The minimum amount of coexistence will be preserved.

But something more positive than that? The kind of cooperation which many of us have been hoping for—hoping for, not just in terms of vague goodwill, but simply because there, and nowhere but there, seems to lie the salvation of the planet. Or a tolerable prospect for most of our fellow human beings. For a brief period—one can even put a date to it, something like 1962 to 1965—there seemed a realistic chance. Now it has become remote. It may not have disappeared; one has to go on hoping that it hasn't disappeared: but everything that has happened in this dark year has pushed it further away.

Everything, both big and little. We all know the obvious examples, the hardening of attitude in both countries, Czechoslovakia, all that we are witnessing: but let me take something which seems less relevant and more innocuous. Student riots in France. There was idealism there. Some university reforms, which ought to have been made a long time ago, have been achieved. But, on the world scale—in the light of the world crisis in which these students are going to live their middle age—they did harm. There is no need to exaggerate the harm, but it is perceptible. Most of the population of France has been thrown back, like the rest of us, to this contemporary state of siege.

That was predictable to anyone with the political intelligence of a newt. The forces which hold our advanced society together are very strong. Only people whose vision of the future is limited to about a week underestimate those forces. But the cost of bringing the forces into play can be very great. You know that in the United States. It tends to make the whole society look inwards. The French society is now looking inwards. And that was the last thing that we—if we have any concern about the world—wanted to happen.

Contemporary France hasn't, of course, made things easy for my country: they tend to regard us as a minor and displeasing extension of an even more displeasing United States. Incidentally I wish General de Gaulle wouldn't insist on referring to us collectively as Anglo-Saxons. I happen to be one: but, purely on grounds of anthropological accuracy, he ought to recollect that he himself is far more likely to be of similar origin—from some related tribe which emerged from the German forests—than are about 60% or 70% of the present population of the United States. Where does he think the northern French came from? But still that doesn't matter. It is a local quarrel. In the broader sense, we need France very badly. As an independent voice which can talk to the Soviet

Union. And in particular which can talk to the East European associates of the Soviet Union. Warsaw, Bucharest, Prague and to some extent Budapest still look to Paris with greater cultural sympathy than they do to New York and London. If ever we can imagine positive collaboration between the superpowers, it will need the kind of mediation which France could help supply. But France has been forced inwards. The independent voice won't be valid for some time. Positive collaboration is that much less likely. Even small things, like the Sorbonne riots, have made their own contribution this year—in the wrong direction. It has never been more important to be tough-minded. There are a lot of gestures, protests, sacrificial actions, which aim at good things, which are in spirit progressive—and which in the result, objectively, end up by being the opposite of progressive.

Sensible persons may very well observe that this positive collaboration between the U.S.A. and the U.S.S.R. is unimaginable any way. To cope with this catastrophe that everyone is predicting needs three separate quantum-jumps in human endeavour—each of them different in kind from anything that men have had the will to do before. The effort that the poor countries have to make on their own account—in particular the major effort to limit population increase. It must come from within the poor countries themselves: it must be matched by a similar restraint in rich countries (that is a psychological necessity): it must have the unqualified support of world opinion, including organized religion, everywhere. Can anyone, sensible persons will ask, believe that *that* will happen?

The first primary agreement between the superpowers to agree to collaborate for humane ends. Wouldn't it take some immediate hostile threat from elsewhere in the galaxy to make that even remotely practicable? Even then, the suspicion, the to-ings and fro-ings, the possibility that hostile intelligences from outer space might perceive the superior virtues of American-type capitalism or Soviet-type communism respectively? For any lesser danger, and a danger ten or twenty years ahead, there is not even the language of discourse in which the superpowers could collaborate. Can anyone believe that *that* will happen?

The third quantum-jump is perhaps even more unlikely than the other two, if that is possible. Assume the wildly improbable, that some sort of collaboration is set going. Then consider the sheer magnitude of the endeavor. To avert the crisis is going to mean sacrifices such as rich countries have never contemplated, except in major war. Much greater than the United States has ever had to bear in any war. There are various estimates of what is required. The most drastic I have seen doesn't come from an American source, though many Americans have told us the size of the problem. This extreme estimate is that, to make the world safe while there is time, the rich countries would have to devote up to 20% of their G.N.P. for a period of ten to fifteen years. Obviously that would mean a radical decrease in military expenditure: it would mean that the standard of living would stay still, and then decrease. It sounds a fantastic estimate: yet I believe it is nearer the truth than more comfortable ones. In the whole of this exercise of seeing our dangers, most of us—and this is certainly true of me—have been complacent. We have been playing at it.

Anyway, the effort needed, both in money and human resources, is immense. Even the United States—granted total benevolence—couldn't do it alone. The U.S.S.R. certainly couldn't. The United States and Western Europe together could make some sort of impact: but that couldn't and wouldn't happen—since it would mean major curbs in military spending—without the U.S.S.R. coming into partnership. Even then, the cost would be very great. Not just in the fairy arithmetic of governments, but in the ordinary lives of ordinary citizens.

Does anyone believe that *that* will happen? We are all selfish. Political memory lasts about a week, the professionals say. Political foresight stretches about another week ahead. To stint ourselves to avoid a disaster in twenty years—what body of people would ever do it? Right. When sensible persons ask me any of those three questions—does anyone believe that that will happen?—the answer is, of course not. For myself, I wish I could: of course I can't.

Now I want you to consider the alternatives, that is, what will probably happen. I am going to suggest three models for the next thirty years. They are all projections, in slightly different directions, from the first part of this discussion.

Model A is the gloomiest. It is, I am afraid, the most likely. The relations between the superpowers will not alter much. They will still coexist, in the sense of avoiding major war. They will spend increasing sums on armaments, anti-ballistic missiles and so on: there will be no greater security for either, and probably not much less. Internally, they will change less than many who live in other countries would expect. This will disappoint both their friends and their enemies. The U.S.S.R. is a very stable society. So, despite all surface appearances, is the U.S.A. Incidentally I know no country where the surface appearance is more misleading. You will go on talking about collective nervous breakdowns: and remain, except for technological irruptions, not so dissimilar to the present state. You will still be burdened with the horrible legacy from the past, for which the ancestors of my countrymen were as much or more to blame as the ancestors of yours. A great many English fortunes were made out of the Negro slave trade—which, in the miscellaneous sordidness of human history, was one of the more sordid passages. And the sins of the fathers have been visited not only on the children, but on someone else's children.

Both the American and Soviet societies will get richer. In many ways, the U.S.A. will get richer faster than the U.S.S.R.: in places the U.S.S.R. will concentrate its priorities effectively, and will keep up. The rest of the advanced world will polarize, as now, towards one or the other of the superpowers. The increase of population all over the rich world may get a little less. In the poor world it won't, except in one or two pockets. Despite local successes, as in India, the food-population collision will duly occur. The attempts to prevent it, or meliorate it, will be too feeble. Famine will take charge in many countries. It may become, by the end of the period, endemic famine. There will be suffering and desperation on a scale as yet unknown. This suffering will be witnessed—since our communications will be even better—by the advanced countries, whose populations will be living better than they are today. It is hard to imagine the psychological and political conditions which will be created by such a gap. Some of us are lucky who won't have to live in them. Without question, the rich populations will feel they are in a state of siege, sometimes in a literal sense: and it may be that our present unease is a shadow thrown backwards from the future.

Model B is a shade more cheerful version of Model A. It depends on several things all going right simultaneously: some, though not dramatic, relaxation between the superpowers: the success of initiatives like Mr. McNamara's: the extension of the Indian agricultural triumph. Some sanguine observers believe that, with immense good fortune, this might conceivably be enough: not enough to avert serious suffering, but enough to tide it over, and give mankind a generation's breathing space to think and plan. I find it hard to believe that they are being realistic. But I respect them for saying, in effect, that in times of trouble it is better to do something rather than nothing. The worst doesn't always happen. That is an old stoical maxim that has taken us all through grim times. The truth is, it may not be adequate for these.

Model C. This is by far the most unlikely of the three: and yet we have to act as though it is more likely than it is. The only decent way to respond to a state of siege is to break out of it. Or at least to try to. Most of us are private citizens, who can only do little things. But the whole world is made up of private citizens, and if they can see the situation, then the situation may be changed. Most of the time, human beings are rapacious and selfish. Some are capable of great nobility, but we can't build on that. Many in rich countries are so selfish that they would—and maybe will—be willing to get richer and use the technological superiority which their riches give them to fight off the hungry millions outside. I for one shouldn't like to live in such a world: and in purely material terms it couldn't be long maintained. But we have to take selfishness for granted. We can also, however, take human intelligence for granted. For all our faults, that has been the strength of the species. It is our best hope now.

We have to tell the facts. We have to make sure that people understand those ominous curves— the curve of population, the curve of food supply. We have to tell what the collision means. And this must be done, not only by high officials like Mr. McNamara, but by private citizens like ourselves. Scientists will have to do it: people in universities are in a strong position to do so: it is the plain duty of churchmen of all kinds.

It is going to need great sacrifices. Including one of the most difficult sacrifices of all, the sacrifice of our rigidities. For, in some ways, a state of siege is comfortable. If we break out, we are going into the harshness of the streets outside. American citizens and Soviet citizens are called upon to face an unfamiliar harshness: the harsh but active assumption that the opposite society is not going to collapse, within foreseeable time. It is no use waiting until the U.S.S.R. becomes capitalist or the U.S.A. communist. If we wait that long, the world population will have doubled, redoubled, re-redoubled, 7 billions, 14 billions, 28 billions. . . . That is the fate which we have to drive home. By the side of that fate, our similarities as human beings ought to be stronger than our differences. Is there any hope that it will prove so?

One hears young people asking for a cause. The cause is here. It is the biggest single cause in history: simply because history has never before presented us with such a danger. It is a very difficult cause to fight, because it will be long-drawn-out, it is going to need using political means for distant ends. We have to stop being trivial. Many of our protests are absurd, judged by the seriousness of the moment in which we stand. We have to be humble and learn the nature of politics. Politics is bound to be in essence short-term. That is no one's fault. Politicians have to cope with the day's tasks. American governments have to try to keep their country safe, in the short term as well as the long. Soviet governments have to do exactly the same. But it is in the nature of politics that the short-term duties come first. It is the duty of all the rest of us, and perhaps most of all the generations which are going to live in what is now the future, to keep before the world its long-term fate. Peace. Food. No more people than the earth can take. That is the cause.

I should be less than honest if I told you that I thought it was likely to succeed. Yet we should be less than human if we didn't try to make it. We live in our time. This is the responsibility of our time, and it is our own. Sometimes I console myself with a piece of rabbinical wisdom:

> *If I am not for myself, who am I?*
> *If I am for myself alone, what am I?*
> *If not now, when?*

C. P. SNOW

THE JOHN FINDLEY GREEN

FOUNDATION LECTURES

OSCAR D. SKELTON, then Undersecretary for Foreign Affairs for the Dominion of Canada. "Some Gains and Losses of the Present Generation"

JOHN LANGDON-DAVIES, author, of London. "Conflict Between Democracy and Fascism in Europe"

FRANCIS B. SAYRE, former High Commissioner to the Philippines. "The Protection of American Export Trade"

T. V. SMITH, Member of Congress and Professor of Philosophy at the University of Chicago. "The Legislative Way of Life"

COUNT CARLO SFORZA of Italy, former Ambassador to China, to Turkey and to France, and subsequently Italian Minister of Foreign Affairs. "The Totalitarian War and After"

SAMUEL GUY INMAN, Lecturer on Latin American Relations at University of Pennsylvania and Yale University. "Pan American Postwar Program"

WINSTON CHURCHILL, former Prime Minister of England, who was introduced by President Harry S. Truman, and accompanied by high dignitaries of the United States. "The Sinews of Peace"

REINHOLD NIEBUHR, Professor of Applied Christian Ethics, Union Theological Seminary, N. Y. "This Nation Under God"

J. C. PENNEY, Merchant. "The Spiritual Basis for Improving Human Relations"

ROSCOE POUND, Dean Emeritus of Harvard Law School. "Justice According to Law"

CHARLES H. MALIK, Ambassador of Lebanon. "The Crisis of Reason"

HARRY S. TRUMAN, former President of the United States. "What Hysteria Does to Us" and "Presidential Papers, Their Importance as Historical Documents"

GUY E. SNAVELY, former Executive Secretary of the Association of American Colleges. "College and Church in America"

STANLEY N. BARNES, Circuit Judge, United States Court of Appeals, Ninth Circuit. "Government and Big Business"

WILLIAM YANDELL ELLIOTT, Williams Professor of Government at Harvard University. "The Uses and Limits of the United Nations in Relation to American Foregn Policy" and "Meeting the Political Strategy and Tactics of the Soviet and Chinese Communist Bloc in the Post-Stalin Period"

DR. EDWARD MC CRADY, Vice-Chancellor and President of the University of the South. "Freedom and Causality"

THE RT. HON. THE VISCOUNT HAILSHAM, Q.C., Lord Privy

Seal, London, England, 1960; "The Iron Curtain, Fifteen Years After"

DR. LIN YUTANG, noted Chinese author, New York City, 1961; "Chinese Humanism and the Modern World" and "Some Good Uses of Our Bad Instincts," in *The Pleasures of a Nonconformist*

HENRY R. LUCE, editor in chief of Time, Life, etc., New York City, 1962; "The Title Deeds of Freedom"

FREDERICK R. KAPPEL, Chairman of Board of American Telephone and Telegraph Company, New York City, 1962; "From the World of College to the World of Work"

MAX KOHNSTAMM, Vice President of Action Committee for the United States of Europe, Brussels, Belgium, 1963; "The European Community and Its Role in the World"

SIR GEORGE PAGET THOMSON, Nobel Prize-winning physicist for work in electrons, Past President, British Association for the Advancement of Science, Cambridge, England, 1964; "Science: The Great Adventure"

ANDRÉ PHILIP, former Minister of Finance in France and leading International Trade Expert, St. Cloud, France, 1965; "Counsel From an Ally"

JOSEPH C. WILSON, President of Xerox Corporation, Rochester, New York, 1965; "The Conscience of Business"

KIM JONG PIL, Chairman, Democratic-Republican Party of Korea, Seoul, Korea, 1966; "Dawn Over Asia" (*Vital Speeches,* vol. xxxiii, November, 1966)

HUBERT H. HUMPHREY, Vice President of the United States, Washington, D. C., 1967; "The Iron Curtain and The Open Door"

FRANC LEWIS MC CLUER, President emeritus, Lindenwood College, St. Charles, Missouri; President, Westminster College, 1933–1947, Fulton, Missouri; "The Continuing Struggle for Freedom"